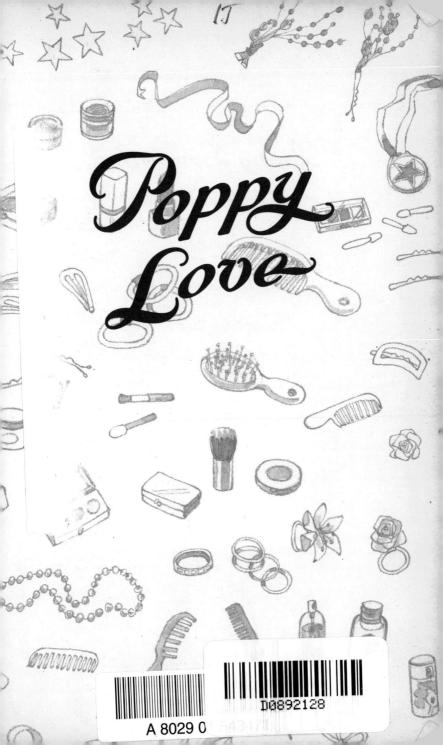

Poppy Love

Poppy Love titles

Poppy Love Steps Out

Poppy Love Faces the Music

Poppy Love Rock 'n' Roll

Poppy Love Star Turn

Poppy Love

Steps Out

NATASHA MAY

illustrated by

SHELAGH McNICHOLAS

WALKER
BOOKS

With thanks to Neil Kelly and the students of
Rubies Dance Centre
N.M.

With thanks to Carolyn, Julia, Kirsty and Ann at
Bell's Dance Centre
S.N.

First published 2009 by Walker Books Ltd
87 Vauxhall Walk, London SE11 5HJ

2 4 6 8 10 9 7 5 3 1

Text © 2009 Veronica Bennett
Illustrations © 2009 Shelagh McNicholas

This book has been typeset in ITC Giovanni

Printed and bound in Great Britain by Clays Ltd, St Ives plc

British Library Cataloguing in Publication Data:
a catalogue record for this book is available from the British Library

ISBN 978-1-4063-1133-4

www.walker.co.uk

Contents

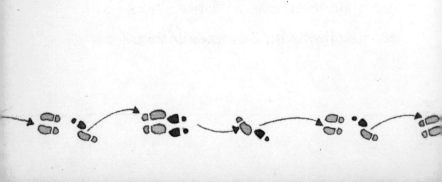

The Lemon-coloured Dress

Poppy Love loved ballroom dancing.

She had been going to the Blue Horizon Dance Studio for two years, and had certificates to show she had passed Grades One, Two and Three. But what Poppy really wanted was to be in a competition. So when her dancing teacher, Miss Johnson, had announced that the dance school was entering the South East Juvenile Ballroom

Dancing Competition, Poppy had been very happy.

On the morning of the competition, Poppy held her lemon-coloured dress against her front and looked in the long mirror. "I want to wear this, Mum," she said.

The dress had a full skirt lined with white material that showed when Poppy twirled. The lemon colour went well with her dark hair, too.

"Do you?" asked Mum, looking up in surprise. She was packing Poppy's dance bag with shoes, socks, make-up, hairpins,  hairspray and the hundred-and-one other things Poppy would need. "I thought you were going to wear your blue dress today."

It was Poppy's turn to be surprised. "But the lemon dress is newer than the blue dress!" she protested. "This is my very first competition, so please can I wear my new dress?"

"Poppy, you know the competition rules," said Mum. "The lemon dress is more of a show dress. It's a bit too fancy to be a competition dress." She looked at Poppy with her head on one side. "And Mrs Heatherington made it a bit looser than the blue one, so that it'll still fit next year. But the blue one fits perfectly now, and it's a very nice dress."

The blue dress was lying on Poppy's bed. It was a soft blue, the colour of the sky, trimmed with lighter blue ribbon, the colour of Poppy's eyes. When Poppy had first seen the dress she'd been thrilled. But however

nice the blue dress was, the lemon dress with its swirling white lining was the dress Poppy wanted to wear.

She decided to have one last try. "Why can't I wear it, Mum?" she asked. "It's not too low or too short, so—"

"But it's still a show dress," interrupted Mum, putting the blue dress into its zip-up cover. And that was that. "Now, please go and tell your brother to hurry up."

Tom's room was next to Poppy's, but Poppy didn't go in. She went down the hall to the sitting-room, where Dad was checking his camera. He looked up and gave her an encouraging smile. "All set for the big day?" he asked. Then he saw that she was almost

crying, and his face changed.
"What's the matter?"

"Mum says my new dress is
a show dress, but it *isn't*!"

"Whoa!" Dad held up his
hand, then patted his knee.
Poppy ran to him and climbed
on his lap. He took her into his arms. "Don't
cry, sweetheart," he said, rocking her gently.
"Today of all days, you should be smiling."

Poppy started to say that she was too upset
to smile, but he stopped her. "What colour is
the dress you want to wear?" he asked.

"Lemon."

"Maybe we can talk to Mum about taking
both dresses. When we get there we'll see
what the other girls are wearing. If lots of
them have lemon-coloured dresses, you'd

11

better wear your other dress so that you stand out from the crowd."

Poppy nodded. This did sound sensible.

"Here," went on Dad, "dry your eyes." He gave her his handkerchief, which was screwed up from being in his pocket, but clean. "All you've got to think about today is dancing beautifully."

Poppy blew her nose. She did feel better. "Thanks, Dad," she said.

The competition was being held in a leisure centre not far from the seaside town of Brighton, where the Love family lived. When they got there, Poppy's partner, Zack Bishop, and his mum had already arrived.

"Zack insisted on leaving so early!" explained Mrs Bishop.

Zack shrugged. "Better to be early than late." He and Tom did a high-five. Then Zack looked at Poppy. "What's up?" he asked.

"My tummy hurts," said Poppy.

"It's probably nerves," said Mrs Bishop. "Perhaps you could think about something besides dancing. What do you like to read, for instance?"

"Books about dancing," said Poppy.

"Oh dear!" said Mrs Bishop, smiling.

Poppy tried to think about arithmetic. Then she tried to think about playing on Brighton's pebbly beach, with the sea breeze tangling up her hair and the edges of the waves tickling her toes. But none of it did any good. "I'm still nervous," she said.

Poppy's Auntie Jill smiled encouragingly. "It's good to be a little nervous before a competition," she said. "It makes you dance better."

Auntie Jill was Mum's younger sister. She used to be a ballroom dancing champion, just like Poppy hoped to be. Now she judged competitions, but today she couldn't be a judge because her niece was in the competition, and it wouldn't be fair to the other dancers.

"Hurry up and get changed," she said to Poppy and Zack. "Miss Johnson will want you to do a warm-up and a run-through."

"A warm-up and a run-through?" echoed Dad. "Sounds like something you'd do to a car engine!"

Poppy knew he was trying to make her feel better by saying something silly. "We have to warm up by doing exercises before we start," she explained, "and then we can run through our dances without hurting ourselves."

The girls' changing room was very crowded. "Dad told me about the dress," Auntie Jill said softly to Poppy while Mum was rummaging in the dance bag. "So what do you think?"

Poppy saw that two girls had bright yellow dresses, and *three* had pale yellow ones. She sighed. "It looks like I'm going to be wearing my blue dress after all," she said.

"Here are your shoes, Poppy," said Mum. She took the blue dress from its cover and admired it. "Lovely!" she said. Then she bent down to give Poppy a kiss. "Friends again?"

Suddenly Poppy felt very happy, and hugged her mum tightly. "Friends!" she told her. Then she put on clean white socks and her silver dancing shoes, and Mum slipped the blue dress over her head. By now, Zack would have on the black trousers, white shirt and black tie all the boys had to wear for competitions.

Auntie Jill began to fix Poppy's hair into a bun. "Ow!" yelled Poppy as a pin dug into her head.

"The pins mustn't fall out," said Auntie Jill, "so hold still and let me get your hair right."

Mum laughed. "Poppy's not a robot, you know," she said.

Poppy did feel a bit like a robot. She had to stand very still while Mum put make-up on her face, and keep her eyes closed while Auntie Jill sprayed her hair. She thought about all the things they'd had to bring today, and the practice shoes, socks, skirts, tops, leggings and tights she had at home. In her dance bag there were spare socks, and a box with sewing thread and needles, safety-pins, elastic and ribbon. Mum had even brought the portable CD player and Poppy's dance music CDs. And this was only her first competition!

But when all the preparation was over, and Mum and Auntie Jill had gone to join Dad and Tom and Mrs Bishop in the audience, Poppy didn't feel like a robot any more. While she and Zack were doing their warm-up and running through their dances, she felt very alive indeed.

"Dance well and enjoy yourselves," said their teacher, Miss Johnson, pinning their numbers on their backs. She didn't say, "Don't let me down," but her face said it for her.

Zack and Poppy looked at each other. They would try their best to dance well *and* not let her down.

When they took up their position on the dance floor and waited for the music to begin, Poppy forgot about everything else in the world except dancing. She forgot about being nervous. She forgot that she was Poppy Love who lived in the Hotel Gemini and went to Linden Tree Junior School. She even forgot that Auntie Jill had promised to take them to the funfair on Brighton pier tomorrow. She just wanted to dance.

The first dance was a cha-cha-cha. This was Poppy's favourite of all the Latin American dances. She loved the rhythm of the music and the wiggly movements that made her skirt flip about. As soon as the dancing started she discovered that being in a competition was a lot of fun. The music was louder than in Miss Johnson's studio, and it felt great to be dancing on a huge floor full of other dancers from lots of dance schools, all doing the cha-cha-cha in their many-coloured dresses and silver shoes.

As there were so many more girls than boys, most girls were dancing with other girls, and the boys danced with lots of different girls over the course of the competition.

After the first round of the cha-cha-cha Poppy did an all-girls event with a girl called Rosie, who had only been in Miss Johnson's Competition Class a few months.

It was a rumba, a slower Latin dance than the cha-cha-cha. Miss Johnson was very pleased when both Poppy and Rosie got through to the next round.

Then Poppy and another girl, Sophie, did a jive – a kicking, jumping dance Poppy liked almost as much as the cha-cha-cha – to some really fast music. Every time Zack danced with another girl Poppy cheered him

on. Poppy and Zack both got through the first round of the cha-cha-cha event.

Then they got through the second round, and the third, and the semi-final.

As the morning went on, Poppy began to feel very hungry and thirsty. Mum passed her a banana and a bottle of water. "Hard work, isn't it?" she said sympathetically.

"It's fun, though!" Poppy drank some water and  began to peel the banana. "What's next?"

Mum looked at the programme. "'Pre-bronze boy-and-girl couple,'" she read. Poppy nodded. She and Zack were in that, as they hadn't taken their bronze medal test yet.

"Three ballroom dances," added her aunt. "Waltz, tango and quickstep."

Poppy loved doing the lively Latin dances, but the ballroom dances appealed to her too, in a different way. It was lovely to be steered smoothly around the floor by Zack, especially in the waltz, which Miss Johnson said he had a special talent for. Poppy knew their

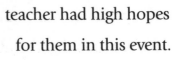

teacher had high hopes for them in this event.

There weren't many couples. As the judges walked round the floor, watching and making notes, Poppy could tell they were studying her and Zack closely. When they finished, she was full of hope that they'd made it through to the next round, which was the final.

When it was time for the final, Mum had her hands over her ears as the numbers were read out. But Dad, Auntie Jill, Tom, Miss Johnson and all her other pupils were listening for their number, 211. When they heard it they began to clap and cheer.

Poppy was very excited when Zack led her out in the last, carefully chosen group. Zack was excited too. "Wow!" he said as the audience applauded. "This is so great!"

While they waited in the middle of the floor, Poppy noticed that none of the girls who had worn pale yellow dresses had got through to the pre-bronze couples final.

For a moment she wondered why, but then the music started and they were off in the waltz.

Poppy and Zack were not placed. The first three couples got trophies, and Poppy and Zack and the other contestants were given little shields. But Poppy wasn't too disappointed. It was their first competition, after all. She stood beside Zack, smiling, while the winners posed for the photographer.

"We were miles better than that couple who came third!" hissed Zack through his smile. "Their tango was awful!"

"Shh!" said Poppy. The announcer was saying something she couldn't hear properly.

"Number two-one-one, Zack Bishop and Poppy Love!" he called.

Zack and Poppy bowed and curtseyed as the audience applauded. "What's going on?" Poppy asked her teacher when they came off the floor and showed Miss Johnson their shields. "Zack was talking and we missed the announcement."

"The head judge says that because the standard is so high, she wants all the finalists to do a show dance after the next event, even if they haven't been placed," explained Miss Johnson. "Isn't that nice?"

Astonished, Poppy stared at her. Then she thought of something. "Where's Mum?"

In the changing room Mum had already got the lemon-coloured dress out. Her eyes were shining. "So," she said, helping Poppy to take off her blue dress, "things turned out pretty well, didn't they?"

Poppy stepped into the lemon-coloured dress. "Yes, they did," she said happily. She looked at her mum's smiling face. Suddenly she realized that Mum and Dad, and Auntie Jill, and even Tom, must have been almost as nervous as she was. "Oh, Mum!" she said. "I'm so glad we brought both the dresses with us!"

Lucky

"Will you tell us about when you were a dancer?" Poppy asked Auntie Jill.

Auntie Jill, Poppy, Tom and Zack were heading downhill to the seafront, where the pier glittered under the bright sun.

"Oh, Poppy, aren't you bored with hearing that story yet?" asked Tom.

"No, I'm not," said Poppy. "I'll never get bored with hearing about dancing."

Tom sighed. "Right, I'm off. Come on, Zack."

Poppy thought Zack might want to hear the story too, but Tom had already started to run down the hill. Zack made a "better do as he says!" face, and followed.

"Wait for me at the entrance to the fair, you two!" called Auntie Jill after the boys.

"Maybe you can tell Zack another time," said Poppy. She looked up at her aunt, thinking how pretty she looked in her white summer dress. "But will you tell me about *your* partner again?" she asked, taking her hand.

Auntie Jill looked at the sea as they walked. "His name was Eduardo," she said, "but everyone called him Eddie. He came from Italy. He was an amazing dancer, and he was very good-looking. He was clever, too. He could do anything."

Poppy loved to hear about Eddie. "Like what?" she asked.

"Well, he was really good at making up steps, and he was very strong." Auntie Jill smiled at the memory. "He would lift me on to his shoulders, or he'd spin me round so fast I could hardly breathe. I had such fun!"

She paused, still looking at the sea. "And he was good to do competitions with, too. He made me feel special even when we didn't win. And we were always laughing. It was as if we were meant to be together."

"What about the trophies you won?" asked Poppy.

"Poppy, you know about the trophies!"

Poppy did. She knew that Auntie Jill and Eddie had won many, many trophies, but Auntie Jill no longer displayed hers.

Years ago, when
Mum and Auntie Jill
lived with Granny
and Grandad in the
flat at the top of the
Hotel Gemini, Auntie
Jill's trophies were in
cabinets in the study.

But when she and
Mum took over the hotel, Auntie Jill gave her
own bedroom to Poppy and moved into the
study, which was too small to be a bedroom
and a trophy room. So the trophies were
packed into boxes and put into the attic.

"But I'd love to hear about them
again," insisted Poppy.

"All right." Auntie Jill took
a breath. "As you know,

ballroom dancing prizes are awarded to each person, so you don't share trophies with your partner. I won a lot before I even met Eddie, and so did he. But together, we started to be really successful." Her eyes took on a dreamy look." We won the British Amateur Latin American Championship three years running, and the European once. I wore sparkly dresses that were more like bikinis – you've seen them in the photos – and after the competitions Eddie and I would go to parties and drink champagne. I was so happy."

"And then?" Poppy reminded her. This was the bit she liked best.

Auntie Jill gave her head a little shake, as if to stop herself dreaming. "And then we won first prize in an international samba festival, in the USA."

"So my auntie was the best samba dancer in the whole world!" said Poppy happily. Excitement rushed through her as she thought of the group samba she and Zack were soon going to be in, at the Southern Counties Festival of Dance. "I love the samba!" she exclaimed.

"So do I," said Auntie Jill. "But that was our only samba trophy. The following year, Eddie went back to Italy."

"Why?" asked Poppy. Although she'd often heard the story of Auntie Jill's career, she'd never before asked what brought it to an end.

Auntie Jill swung Poppy's hand a little. "Oh, we'd been partners for eight years, and Eddie wanted to do something new," she said. "He ended up marrying an Italian girl and they started a dance school in Italy."

"Didn't *you* want to marry him?" Poppy asked in a small voice.

"I think so, yes." Auntie Jill's voice was small too. "But anyway, I gave up dancing because I couldn't find a partner who was as good as Eddie. So I became a judge and an examiner."

She sighed a little, remembering. Then she said, more briskly, "Soon after that, your mum and I took over the hotel. Then she met your dad." She thought for a moment. "But I'll get the trophies out again one day. Perhaps when I get a place of my own."

Poppy tried to imagine what life in the flat at the top of the Hotel Gemini would be like without Auntie Jill. "When will that be?" she asked.

"Oh, goodness knows," said Auntie Jill, still swinging

Poppy's hand. "I love living with all of you, but … I'd like to get married one day."

"Get married?" asked Poppy in surprise. But then, Auntie Jill was several years younger than Mum, and very attractive.

"Yes," said Auntie Jill, beginning to laugh. "You and Tom might even have cousins some day! But we're getting ahead of ourselves. I'm not even seeing anyone!"

They were almost at the funfair. Poppy could see Tom and Zack standing under the huge sign advertising the fair. "Will you get a house with a garden?" she asked her aunt. "So that you can have a puppy?"

Auntie Jill laughed. "You and your puppy! I think I'm going to have to call you Puppy, not Poppy!"

"Will you, though?"

Auntie Jill squeezed her hand. "Of course. And you can come and play with the puppy whenever you want. Now, where are those boys?"

The funfair was certainly fun. Poppy ate some candy floss and an ice cream. Then she screamed until she was almost sick all over Zack on the cup-and-saucer spinner. She went on the rollercoaster with Tom and was frightened, but in an exciting way. Tom held on to her all the way through the ride, though not because *he* was frightened, of course.

When Poppy had spent all the money Dad had given her, she and Auntie Jill strolled about in the warm sunshine, giggling as they tried on cheap hats and sunglasses. Then, just as they began to wonder where the boys had got to, Poppy saw Lucky.

He was the sweetest toy puppy possible. He had big eyes and floppy ears, and he lay with his nose on his paws exactly like a real dog. He was in a glass case with lots of other cuddly toys, and you had to put money in a slot and use the handles on the front of the machine to move a grabber to get the toy you wanted.

"Auntie Jill…" Poppy caught hold of her aunt's wrist. "I haven't got any more money, but please, *please* can I have a go at this?"

"Well, all right," said Auntie Jill, reaching for her purse.

Poppy pointed to Lucky. "I'm going to try and get that puppy. Isn't he lovely? I'm going to call him Lucky."

"You've got to win him first!"
laughed Auntie Jill.

Poppy put the coins in the slot and
took hold of the handles. The grabber
started moving, but it was jerky
and hard to control. Poppy
managed to get hold of Lucky,
but dropped him before she
could get him out. Then the
grabber stopped.

"Can I try again?" she
asked. "Just once more?"

But once more wasn't enough to win
Lucky. Disappointed, Poppy turned away
from the machine.

"What's going on?"

It was Tom. He and Zack had appeared,
both hot-looking from the try-your-strength

machine. Poppy decided not to ask which of them had turned out to be stronger.

"Poppy's fallen in love with that puppy," explained Auntie Jill. "She's tried to catch him, but it's too difficult."

"Let me have a go," said Zack, taking coins from his pocket.

"Bet you can't do it," said Tom.

"Bet I can." Zack took hold of the handles and moved the grabber carefully towards Lucky. It picked up the puppy by its ear. Zack moved the handles and the grabber lifted the puppy slowly over the side of the glass. Then, suddenly, Lucky fell out of its clutches and straight into Poppy's arms.

"Thank you, Zack!"

"It wasn't so hard," he told Poppy. "I'm taller than you, so I can see better."

"Lucky!" said Poppy, hugging the toy puppy. "You're going to bring us so much luck!" Then she realized something, and held the puppy out towards Zack. "You won him," she said shyly. "So he's yours."

"I won him for *you*, Pop," said Zack. He ignored Tom, who was holding his stomach, pretending to be helpless with laughter.

"And it was a very nice thing to do, Zack," said Auntie Jill. "Now, stand still and I'll take a photo of you all."

She held up her camera and looked through it. As she tried to get the three children and Lucky into the shot, she took a step backwards.

"Look out!" someone cried. A man behind Auntie Jill, dressed in shorts and sandals, stumbled as he tried to get out of her way.

Auntie Jill whirled round, her curls flying round her head. "Oh, I'm so sorry! Did I hurt you?"

The man had light hair and spectacles, and looked about the same age as Poppy's dad. Beside him stood two boys, both younger than Poppy. They were looking at her and the two older boys curiously. "No, I was too quick!" joked the man. "Look, why don't I take a picture of all four of you?"

"That's very kind," said Auntie Jill. She gave him the camera and the man took the photo.

"My name's Simon," he said to Auntie Jill as he handed back the camera. "And these are my nephews, Ben and Tom."

"And this is *my* nephew Tom!" said Auntie Jill, putting her hand on Tom's shoulder.

He grinned at the younger Tom, who grinned back.

"And this is my niece, Poppy, and our friend, Zack," went on Auntie Jill.

"And your name is…?" asked Simon.

Auntie Jill's cheeks went pink. Poppy thought it made her look prettier. "Jill," she said.

Simon fished in his shirt pocket and handed Auntie Jill a small white card. "I own this restaurant, Forrester's," he said. "If you'd like to come in for a meal, or even a drink, just call me. It'll be on the house."

"Thank you." Auntie Jill looked at the card. "Actually, you and I are in the same business."

"Are we?" asked Simon. His eyes behind his spectacles looked very interested. The younger boy, Ben, was pulling his uncle's hand, but Simon took no notice. "Do you own a restaurant too?"

"My sister and I own the Gemini Hotel," Auntie Jill told him.

"Oh, in Paget Street. I know it." Simon looked at her a little longer. Then he seemed to realize that his nephews were restless. "All right, Ben," he said. He looked awkwardly at the ground, then at the children. "Well ... it was nice to meet all of you. I hope to see you again. Goodbye."

"Goodbye," said Auntie Jill. "And thanks very much for this."

When Simon had gone she turned to the children. Her face wasn't pink anymore, but she looked pleased. "They were nice, weren't they? Now, who'd like a drink? Let's go to that café."

"How can a meal be on the house?" asked Poppy. She'd been puzzling about this ever since Simon had said it. "Which house did he mean?"

"It isn't a real house," Auntie Jill explained. "It just means we won't have to pay if we go to his restaurant."

Tom had a question too. "How did you know he wasn't going to steal the camera? Mum and Dad are always saying watch out for thieves and pickpockets in a fairground."

Auntie Jill thought. "I suppose he just looked honest. And he had children with him. But…" she said, poking Tom lightly in the back as they went into the café, "…you're quite right. I should have been more careful. I must have not been thinking what I was doing."

"I wonder why?" muttered Tom.

Poppy dug him in the ribs. "Ssh!" she said. Then, in a louder voice, "It's not every day you get a free meal, is it? Or meet some nice new people? Lucky's already been lucky, so just imagine how much luck he's going to bring us in our dancing!"

Carnival Dance

The weather was hot. The studio was hot.
And Poppy was hot. Although she was
wearing cool practice clothes – a short skirt
and a top with thin straps – she could see
in the mirror that covered the studio wall
that her face was very red. And she was only
doing her warm-up exercises.

"What if it's as hot as this on Saturday?"
she asked Zack.

"Don't remind me," said Zack, holding the ballet *barre* and stretching the backs of his legs. "I've got to wear a long-sleeved shirt, remember?"

Every afternoon for the past week, Poppy, Zack and the other children had been going to the Blue Horizon Dance Studio to rehearse their routine for the Southern Counties Festival of Dance. Poppy had longed for the day for ages, but now it seemed to be coming up on them very quickly. Suddenly, there were only two days left.

She joined Zack in his stretching exercises, feeling pleased that he was her partner. He loved dancing as much as she did, and though he joked around sometimes like all boys, when he needed to be serious, he was. It was strange, but the first time she danced with Zack the steps suddenly seemed easier, and Poppy's dancing quickly improved. Miss Johnson noticed too. She looked at them with excitement on her face, saying, "I think we've got something here, you two!"

Zack and the other boys in the samba dance, Sam and Luke, were the only boys in Miss Johnson's Competition Class. Sam and Zack had been in the class since before Poppy joined it, over a year ago, but Luke was newer. He'd danced with Poppy in class, of course, but hadn't spoken to her much. He seemed shy. But he threw himself into the dances with all his heart, as if he preferred to speak with his feet rather than his mouth.

"Right, everyone," said Miss Johnson, clapping her hands. "You should be warmed up now. So let's samba!"

The samba was a Latin American dance set to fast music, with a strong drumbeat. Miss Johnson said it was the dance of Brazilian carnivals, where everyone danced at a great big party held in the street. It not only had backwards, forwards and sideways steps, but the dancers had to remember to bounce up and down to the rhythm of the music with every step. They also had to do turns and promenades, which meant dancing while moving forwards with their partner. And they had to do Poppy's favourite step of all, the samba roll. In this, Zack stood behind her, holding one of her hands near her hip and the other outstretched, and then they leaned forwards and backwards while going round and round.

Miss Johnson watched carefully while the children did the routine over and over again. Once in a while she corrected them, but mostly she just watched. The children knew the dance perfectly by now. But Miss Johnson wanted it *more* than perfect. Poppy remembered how scary she thought Miss Johnson was going to be on her first day at dance class. But she wasn't scary at all. She was kind, and didn't shout. She was nice-looking, too, and had dark eyes which shone when her dancers did their steps properly, and clouded when they didn't.

Suddenly, she stopped the music and began to walk about the studio, frowning. Her eyes had their clouded look.

"Here she goes," whispered Zack in Poppy's ear. "I bet she'll change it, just when we've finally learnt it."

Miss Johnson stopped. She still looked very thoughtful. "It's missing something," she said. "It needs to be more like a real carnival dance." Then her eyes started to shine. "I know! We'll start it with cartwheels!"

The children were surprised. "Can you really have cartwheels in dancing?" asked Sam.

"Well, they're not normally in the samba," replied Miss Johnson, "and they wouldn't be allowed in a competition. But this performance is for a show, so the rules don't matter.

I want the beginning to be as dramatic as possible." She looked at Poppy and the other two girls. "Can you all do cartwheels?"

"I can," said Cora.

"Me too," said Sophie.

Poppy looked at Cora, who was a little older than her, and had dark curly hair. Then she looked at Sophie, with her round face and big smile. She liked both girls, and didn't want to let them down. But she couldn't do a cartwheel.

"What about you, Poppy?" asked Miss Johnson.

Poppy shook her head. "No, I can't. And I don't think I can learn in two days," she said.

"Yes you can!" said Cora.

"We'll teach you!" added Sophie. "It's not so hard, once you get the idea."

Everyone was looking at Poppy, except Luke, who was Cora's partner. Poppy wondered if *he* could do a cartwheel. "OK, I'll have a go," she said.

"Good girl," said Miss Johnson, patting her shoulder. "The trick is to think of yourself as a wheel, and not bend your legs. Show us, girls."

Sophie and Cora showed Poppy what to do. But when Poppy tried, her legs wouldn't go up high enough, or stay straight. And she kept putting both her hands on the floor at the same time, which Miss Johnson said was wrong.

"One hand first, Poppy, just before the other one," she instructed. "And *up* go the legs."

But Poppy's legs didn't
go up. She looked more
like a frog hopping
than a wheel turning.
And she was getting
very, very hot.

"Let's do the routine again," suggested Miss
Johnson. "We'll keep it as it is for now." She
went to the CD player. "Everyone ready?"

They did it again. But somehow, the
excitement had gone out of the dance. Poppy
knew the others were disappointed about
the cartwheels. She felt as if she'd spoiled
everything. Biting her lip, she held back tears.

Then she felt Luke's hand on her arm. Shy
Luke was taller and thinner than Zack, with
freckles on his nose and cheeks. "You can do
it," he said.

"I don't think so," said Poppy, trying to stop her voice trembling. "I'm afraid I'll fall and hurt myself."

Luke took a deep breath. "I'll tell you a secret. When we had to climb ropes at school, everyone laughed at me because I was afraid to do it." He'd gone pink under his freckles. "Then the PE teacher put some bean bags – you know, the big ones you sit on – underneath the ropes, and I just went and climbed right to the top without even looking down."

This was more than Poppy had ever heard him say. And while she'd been almost crying a minute before, now she was almost smiling. "You mean you could do it because you knew you wouldn't get hurt if you fell?" she asked.

"That's right," replied Luke. "And there are mats in the storeroom. Miss Johnson uses them when she teaches yoga."

"Thanks, Luke!"

Poppy had a word with Miss Johnson, who began to smile. "What a good idea, Poppy!"

"Luke thought of it," said Poppy.

Miss Johnson nodded, and turned back to the others. "Come on, everyone, help me get the mats out!"

Poppy tried again. She still couldn't do the cartwheel properly but, just as Luke had said, the mats made her feel more confident. Over and over again she practised. And suddenly, just when she felt like giving up, something seemed to click. She knew exactly what to do. She put her left hand down before her right hand, keeping her arms straight.

She flung her legs up, and they too stayed straight. Her right foot came down before her left foot, and before she knew it she was up on her feet again.

The others applauded, and Cora hugged Poppy. "See?" she said gleefully. "I just *knew* you could do it! And you looked really good, too!"

"Well done, Poppy!" said Miss Johnson. "Now come on, you lot, let's put the cartwheels into the routine!"

This was quite difficult to do. The girls had to cartwheel across the floor, then back again, before beginning to dance in time to the music. At first Cora, Sophie and Poppy couldn't get the timing right, and kept finishing their cartwheels at the wrong moment. But Miss Johnson counted the beats loudly while Zack, Luke and Sam stamped their feet on every count. In the end the three girls all ended up in the right place at the right time.

After the girls had done the cartwheels, they had to dance in a line with the boys behind them. Then the girls and boys formed into three couples and circled the floor, doing samba steps with the special moves Miss Johnson had made up.

"And *roll* those hips, and *stretch* that arm, and *think* about those feet!" Miss Johnson called as the children danced. Her eyes darted about, missing nothing. "Zack, watch your head – it's going *left* when your arm goes *right*, remember? Don't look at Poppy till the *next* beat. That's better!"

"How can I watch my head when my eyes are *in* my head?" panted Zack.

"You know what I mean!" said Miss Johnson.

At the end Zack sank dramatically to the floor. "We're worn out!" he groaned. "Isn't it time to go home *yet*?"

"Almost," said Miss Johnson, looking at the clock. "Do it one last time, then we'll stop for today. Come on, Zack."

Slowly, Zack got up and went to his position. Miss Johnson pressed the PLAY button on the CD player. "Go for it!" she called.

Poppy went for it.
She loved doing the
dance. Usually she
and the other girls had
to do the boy's part
of all the dances as
well as the girl's. No
one minded, as it was all
part of ballroom dancing, and

none of them would have
changed it for the world.
But Poppy was thrilled
to be dancing in a
routine with three
girls and three boys
for a change, just
like the grown-up
dancers on TV.

By the time they finished she felt hotter than she'd ever felt in her life. But she was even more excited about the dance than she'd been before. It was going to be brilliant! And Mum was going to videotape it, so they could watch it over and over again.

Miss Johnson put her bag over her shoulder. "I hope the weather's a bit cooler by Saturday," she said as they left the studio, "although it will be nice to have some sunshine, as the performance is outdoors." She looked round all the children, smiling happily. "Well done, everyone. You've all worked very hard this afternoon, especially Poppy. Same time tomorrow, then! Don't be late!"

Out in the street, Poppy's mum was standing by her car with Mrs Bishop. They waved when they saw the children.

"All finished?" asked Mum. "Goodness, you look like you need a drink! I've got some water with me."

"How did it go?" asked Mrs Bishop.

"Miss Johnson's changed the dance," said Zack. "I knew she would."

"And how has it changed?" asked his mum.

"It's better," said Poppy. "The girls are doing cartwheels, so it's much more like a carnival dance."

Mum looked puzzled. "I didn't think you could do a cartwheel, Poppy."

"I can now!" Poppy told her. "Cora and Sophie helped me. And Luke did, too."

Mum smiled, and reached for the water. "I bet the dance looks spectacular," she said as she unscrewed the top. "I can't wait for Saturday!"

"Me too," said Poppy. "It's going to be a day to remember for ever!"

Taking the Crowd to Brazil

It was the day of the Southern Counties
Festival of Dance.

The festival was held on the seafront in
Eastbourne, a town further along the coast
from Brighton. The dance school across
the road was being used for rehearsing and
dressing. When Poppy and her mum arrived
there, Poppy looked around in amazement.
She had never in her life seen so many

people wearing so many different kinds of dance costumes.

"Look at all the *incredible* dresses, Mum!" she said.

A group of girls, still dressed in their ordinary clothes with their dance bags over their shoulders, were walking through the hall carrying dresses so heavily embroidered with intricate patterns, and so brightly coloured, they shone like jewels. Each dress was slightly different from the others, though all were in the same style, and all were equally beautiful.

"Those are traditional Irish dancing costumes," explained Mum. "Lots of different countries are taking part in this festival.

You'll be able to watch the
dancing when the samba's over.
Now, where are the others?"

Miss Johnson had arranged
for Poppy and the other
children to meet in one
of the studios for a final
rehearsal. When Mum
pushed open the double
doors, a strange sound met Poppy's ears.
The studio was being shared by a great many
dancers, so several different kinds of music
were all playing at once. In one corner a
Spanish flamenco troupe was stamping and
clapping, and in another a line of women
in checked dresses were doing a clog dance.
Their feet moved so fast Poppy could
hardly see them.

"Hello!" Miss Johnson came towards them, smiling widely and holding Cora by the hand. Cora gave Poppy a friendly smile, but Poppy found she couldn't smile back. Her stomach felt as if someone had tied it in a knot.

Mum went off to get a space in the changing room and Miss Johnson led Poppy to where the others were doing warm-up exercises. Zack looked as if his stomach was in a knot, too. "Are you OK?" she asked him.

"I think so." He looked around the crowd of brightly dressed figures. "But I didn't feel like this when we did that competition, Pop. Maybe because that was all children. Most of these people are adults."

"We're not competing against them, though," said Poppy. "And look, those Irish dancers are only young girls."

Zack sighed. "I still kind of wish it was over."

"You'll be all right," said Poppy encouragingly. "You always are."

They finished warming up and did the routine twice. "Very good," said Miss Johnson. "But I think we'd better have one last practice when you've got your costumes on, don't you?"

Poppy was glad. She never felt a dance was really happening until she got the dress on. As she followed the others to the girls' changing room, her stomach began to feel better.

The changing room was very crowded. Mum was chatting to Cora's and Sophie's mothers, surrounded by shoeboxes and vanity cases, mirrors and hairdryers and screwed-up tissues, and costumes of every description. "You look almost as pink as your dress!" she said when she saw Poppy.

Poppy looked at the three samba dresses hanging on the rail. Her own was bright pink, while curly-haired Cora had a green one and Sophie, whose fair hair framed her always-smiling face, was in orange.

All the dresses were of a similar style, with skirts that were short at the front and longer at the back, so that they looked like the tail of a fish. They had frills all the way down the back, which rippled when the girls did the hip-rolling samba moves. It had taken Mrs Heatherington a long time to sew those frills, so Mum and Poppy had helped her by sticking the sequins on the dress. Cora's mum had made little decorations with sequined feathers for the girls to wear in the side of their hair, and they all had white socks and silver shoes.

"I can't wait to get this on!" exclaimed Sophie, holding her dress against her front. "I'm so excited!"

Poppy was excited too, though her stomach still felt tight. It was hard to stand still while Mum sprayed her with fake tan. Even when she was sitting down having her make-up done she kept fidgeting, and the eye-liner pencil kept slipping. "Poppy!" said Mum. "I know you're excited but you must keep still!"

"I wish Auntie Jill could have come," said Poppy as Mum brushed her hair.

"So do I, sweetheart," said Mum. "But someone has to run the hotel."

Poppy knew this was true. Her family never had any time off during the summer, because it was the busiest season of the year. She sometimes wished they could go on holiday like everyone else, although living in Brighton was almost like being on holiday anyway. This year, it had been so hot that the beach was covered with sunbathers and the pier was almost too crowded to walk along.

While Mum put her hair in a bun and fixed the pink decoration into it, Poppy noticed Lucky, her lucky toy puppy, peeping out from under a pile of Sophie's clothes. She picked him up and held him to her chest. She didn't talk to him out loud – she only did that when she was by herself – but in her head she told him that he had to bring lots of luck today. For her, but also for Zack, who had sounded so glum when he'd seen all the other dancers. It was only because of Zack that she even had Lucky, after all.

"Will you bring Lucky over to the stage and hold him while we're dancing?" Poppy asked her mum. "He'd like to watch us, I know he would."

"You funny thing," said Mum, shaking her head. She was smiling, though. "Sometimes I think you believe that toy is real."

When they were dressed, the girls went back to the studio. Poppy felt a little shy. She'd never been so dressed-up before, even for fancy dress parties. But she soon forgot her shyness when she saw Miss Johnson's face.

"You all look wonderful!" she said, her eyes shining. The boys had black shirts and trousers with bright bands round their waist to match their partners' dresses. "Ready?"

She started the music, and they went through the dance one more time. "Those dresses look fabulous when you girls shake your hips!" she said. Then she held out her arms in a "gather round" gesture. "Now, listen. This is a show dance," she said seriously, "so you don't have to worry about pleasing judges. But you have to make it as entertaining as you can."

On her face was the look Poppy knew well. It meant, "Don't let me down."

When she patted each child's shoulder and said, "Take the crowd to Brazil!" Poppy knew what they had to do. You couldn't take the crowd to Brazil unless you put every last scrap of effort into the samba.

While they were crossing the road Poppy could hear Zack whistling under his breath. She knew he only did this when he was nervous. But Poppy's own nerves had gone. She just wanted to dance.

They took their positions on the platform that had been built on the grass. The audience applauded as the name of their dancing school was read out over the loudspeakers. The boys bowed and the girls curtseyed, then they got into their positions for the start of the routine.

After weeks and weeks of work, everything would be over in two and a half minutes. Poppy's heart pounded as she heard the first beats of the samba music come over the loudspeakers, and the dance began.

Then there was a disaster.

The three girls did their cartwheels diagonally across the stage. But because Miss Johnson had put the cartwheels into the dance two days before, they'd practised them in costume only once. As Poppy reached the corner and turned to do her next cartwheel, the heel of her shoe caught in the fishtail of her dress.

She heard the crowd gasp, then groan. Mrs Heatherington's neat stitching came apart as Poppy tried desperately to keep her balance. She managed not to fall over, but her foot had gone through the hole her shoe had made in the skirt, making the skirt flap around her legs like loose trousers. Poppy knew that all her skirt-shaking moves would be spoilt unless she got her foot out. But she couldn't do this without stopping the dance.

No one ever, ever stops a dance once it has started! Miss Johnson had told them this so many times Poppy didn't even consider stopping. She picked up the next beat of the music, dancing to the front of the stage with Zack behind her, then she turned, took his hand and tried to smile as they began the backwards-and-forwards samba steps. Continuing the dance as if nothing had happened was very hard when her beautiful pink dress had unexpectedly turned into trousers.

When they struck the finishing pose the applause was very loud. The audience was clapping especially hard out of sympathy, and Poppy was grateful to them. But there was no avoiding the truth: her mishap had ruined the dance they'd worked for so long to get right. And to make things worse, Mum had filmed it all! Lucky hadn't been so lucky after all.

As they left the stage she couldn't help beginning to cry. But then she saw Miss Johnson speaking to the man with the headset who organized the Southern Counties Festival of Dance. Miss Johnson's hands were fluttering this way and that. Poppy wondered what she could be saying to him.

The next performers, who were going to do a German folk dance, started up the steps to the stage. But then there was an announcement. The man with the headset had taken the microphone. "Who wants to see that wonderful samba again?" he asked.

The crowd roared. Yes, they most certainly did.

Miss Johnson rushed towards Poppy, a safety-pin in each hand. In a flash she'd pinned the pink dress so that it no longer had a hole and looked like a dress again. Then she practically pushed Poppy back up the steps onto the stage.

The dance went perfectly. When they had finished, the applause went on for so long they had to bow and curtsey six times. And when Poppy left the stage, with Zack's hand holding hers so tightly it hurt, she began to cry all over again. Not because Zack was hurting her hand, but because of the look on their teacher's face.

"My little stars!" exclaimed Miss Johnson, hugging first Poppy, then the other girls, then the boys. "Come on, you've got to pose for the photographer. Dry your tears, Poppy."

"Dry *your* tears?" muttered Zack as they got into a line. "She's almost crying herself!"

Miss Johnson might be in tears, but she was very, very happy. The six children had taken the crowd to Brazil and back again – twice!

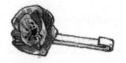

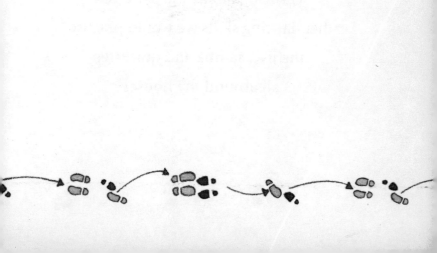

Natasha May loves dance of all kinds. When she was a little girl she dreamed of being a dancer, but also wanted to be a writer. "So writing about dancing is the best job in the world," she says. "And my daughter, who is a dancer, keeps me on my toes about the world of dance."

Shelagh McNicholas loves to draw people spinning around and dancing. Her passion began when her daughter, Molly, started baby ballet classes, "and as she perfected her dancing skills we would practise the jive, samba and quickstep all around the house!"